SEP   2012

WELCOME TO
PASSPORT TO READING
A beginning reader's ticket to a brand-new world!

Every book in this program is designed to build read-along and read-alone skills, level by level, through engaging and enriching stories. As the reader turns each page, he or she will become more confident with new vocabulary, sight words, and comprehension.

These PASSPORT TO READING levels will help you choose the perfect book for every reader.

READING TOGETHER
Read short words in simple sentence structures together to begin a reader's journey.

READING OUT LOUD
Encourage developing readers to sound out words in more complex stories with simple vocabulary.

READING INDEPENDENTLY
Newly independent readers gain confidence reading more complex sentences with higher word counts.

READY TO READ MORE
Readers prepare for chapter books with fewer illustrations and longer paragraphs.

This book features sight words from the educator-supported Dolch Sight Word List. Readers will become more familiar with these commonly used vocabulary words, increasing reading speed and fluency.

For more information, please visit www.passporttoreadingbooks.com, where each reader can add stamps to a personalized passport while traveling through story after story!

Enjoy the journey!

Little, Brown and Company

Hachette Book Group
237 Park Avenue, New York, NY 10017
Visit our website at www.lb-kids.com

LB kids is an imprint of Little, Brown and Company. The LB kids name and logo
are trademarks of Hachette Book Group, Inc.

The publisher is not responsible for websites (or their content)
that are not owned by the publisher.

First Edition: April 2012

ISBN 978-0-316-17860-0

Library of Congress Control Number: 2011935088

10 9 8 7 6 5 4 3 2

CW

Printed in the United States of America

MARVEL SUPER HERO SQUAD™

SUPER HERO SHOWDOWN!

by Lucy Rosen
illustrated by Dario Brizuela
inks by Andres Ponce • coloring by Franco Riesco

LITTLE, BROWN & COMPANY
LB kids

Attention,

all Super Hero Squad fans!

Look for these items when you read this book.

Can you spot them all?

JUGGERNAUT

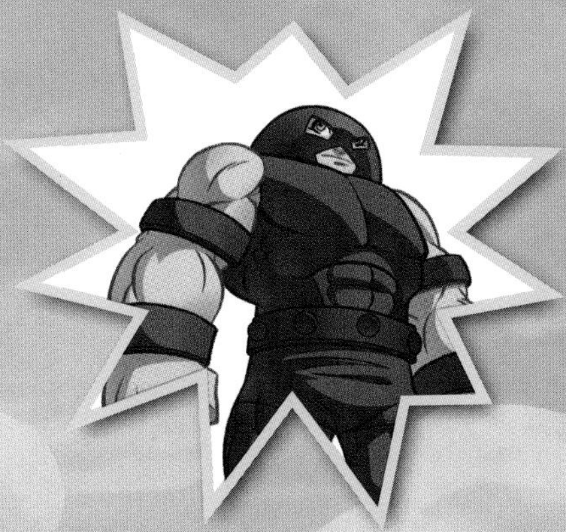

MALLET

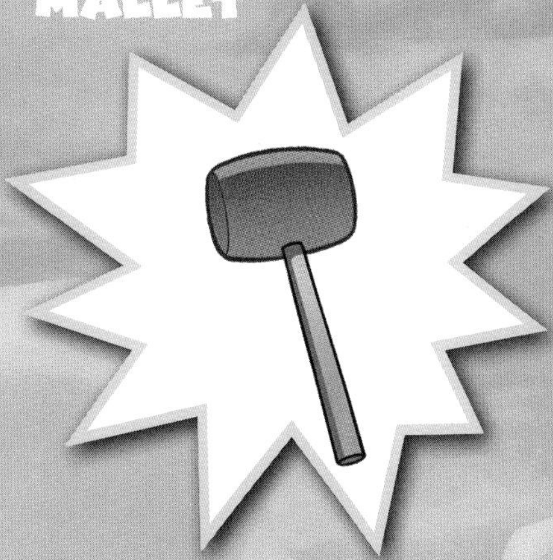

BOULDER

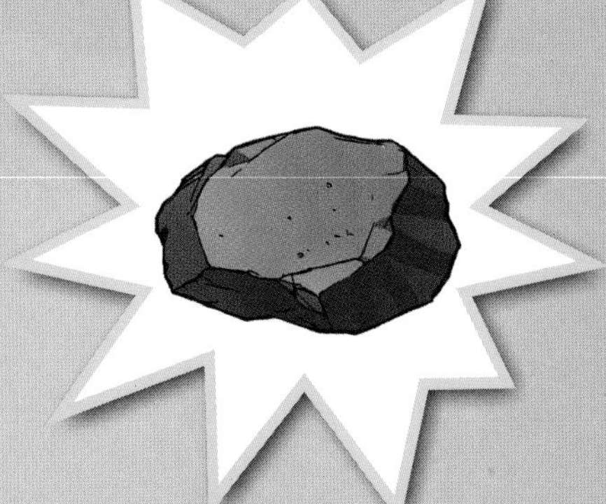

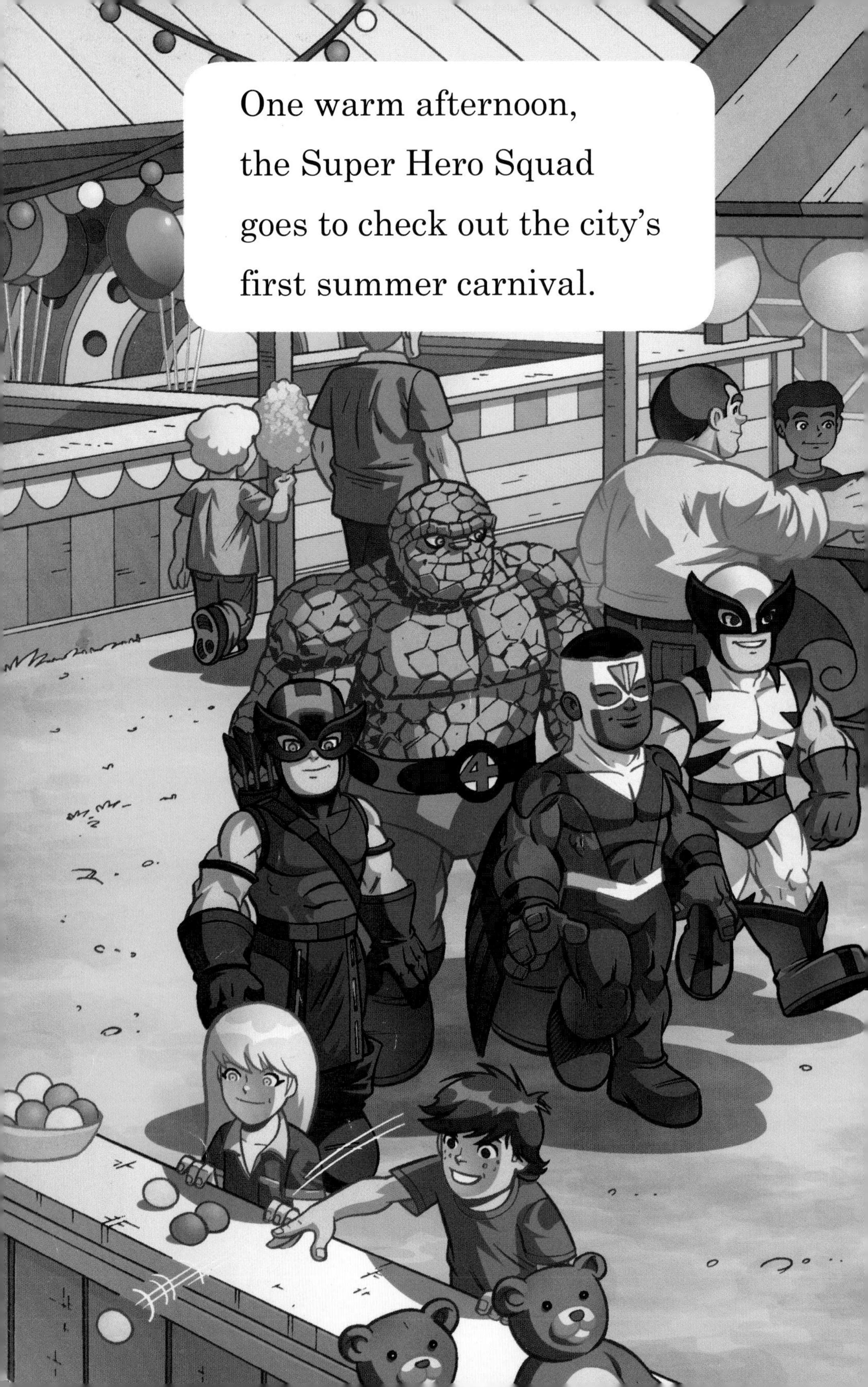

One warm afternoon,
the Super Hero Squad
goes to check out the city's
first summer carnival.

Luke Cage wants to try
the strength test.
"Step right up!" says Iron Man.
Luke takes the mallet.

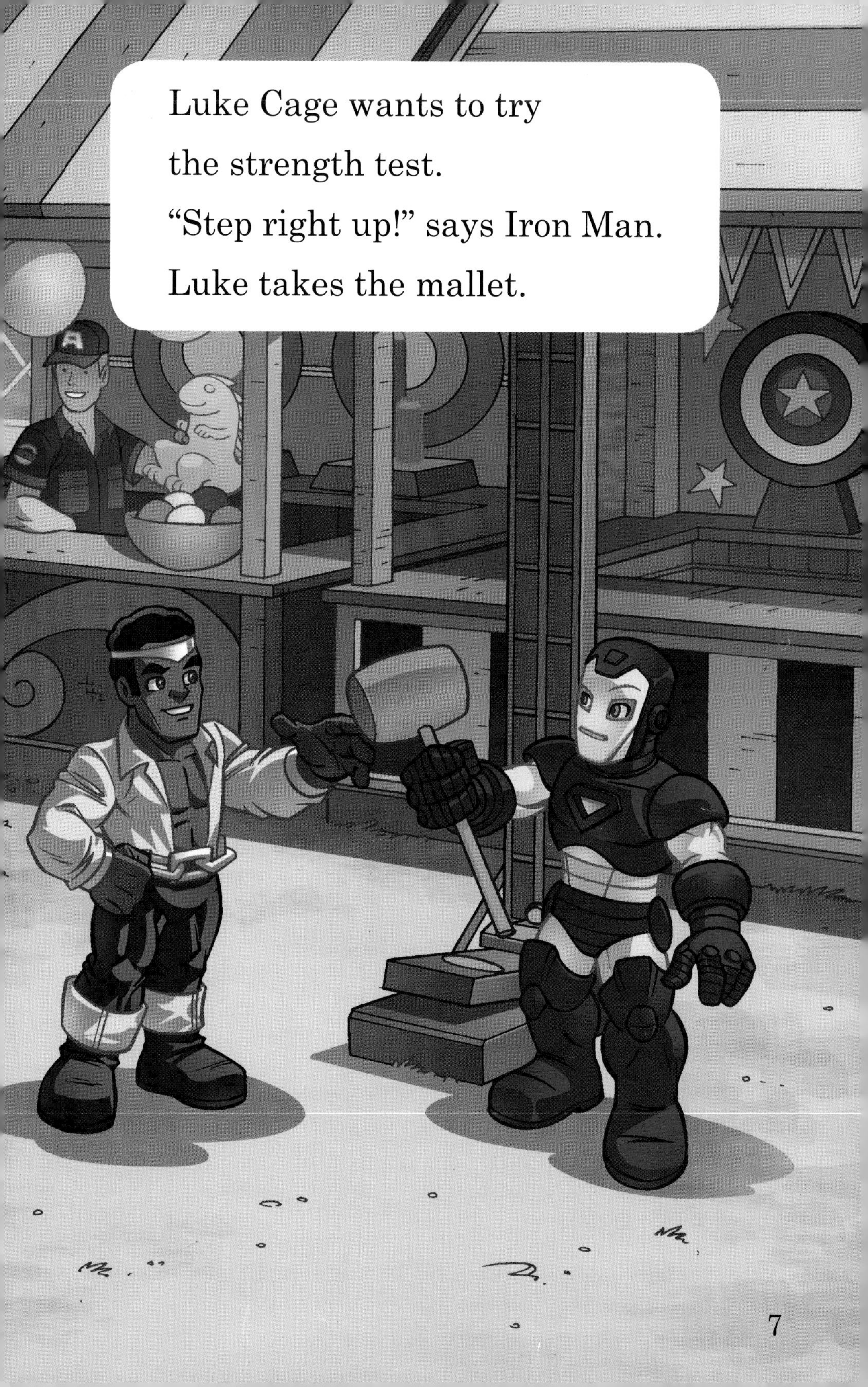

"Piece of cake," brags Luke.
"Strongman contests are
kind of my thing!"

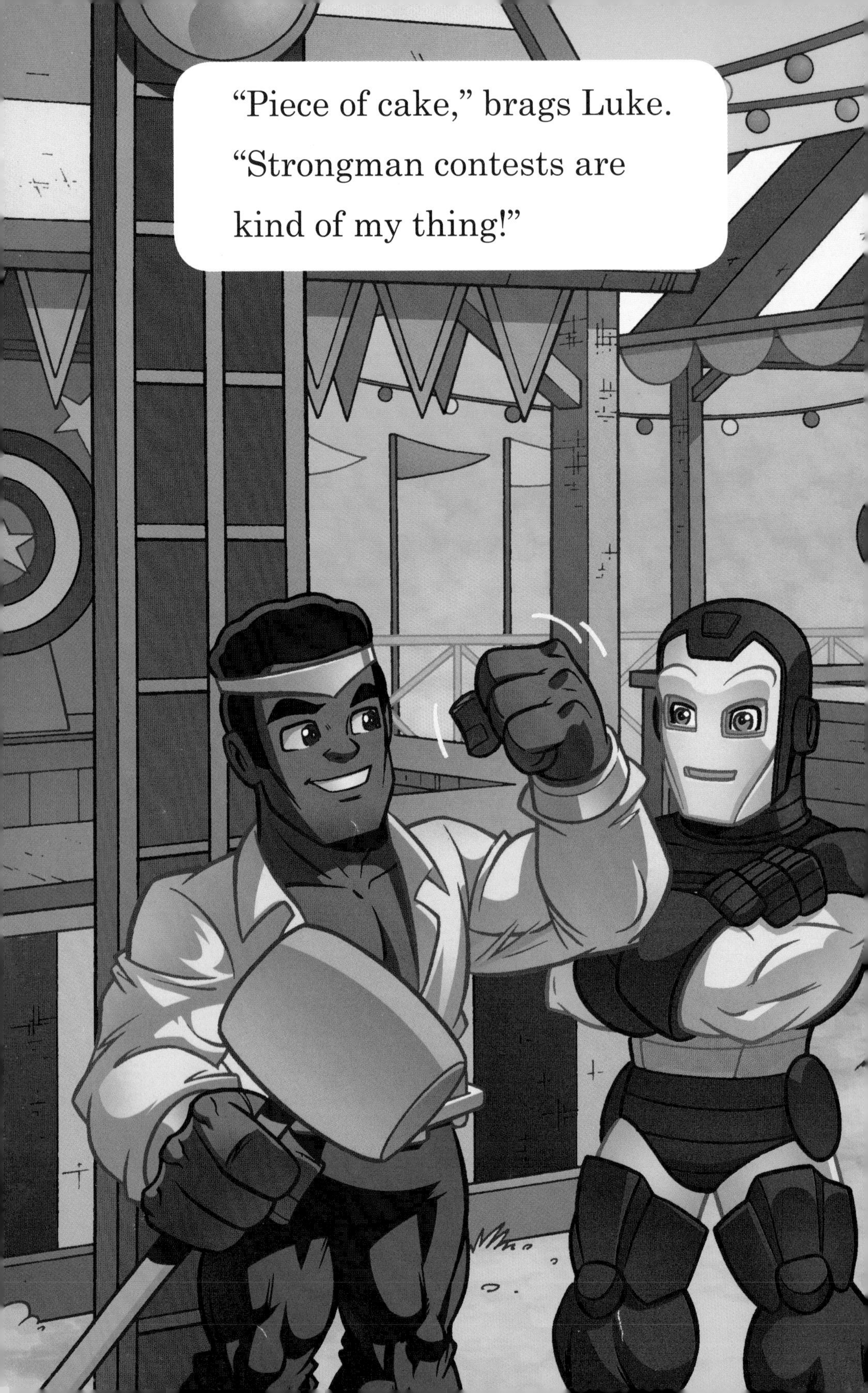

"I do not think so, Cage,"
someone growls.
It is Juggernaut!

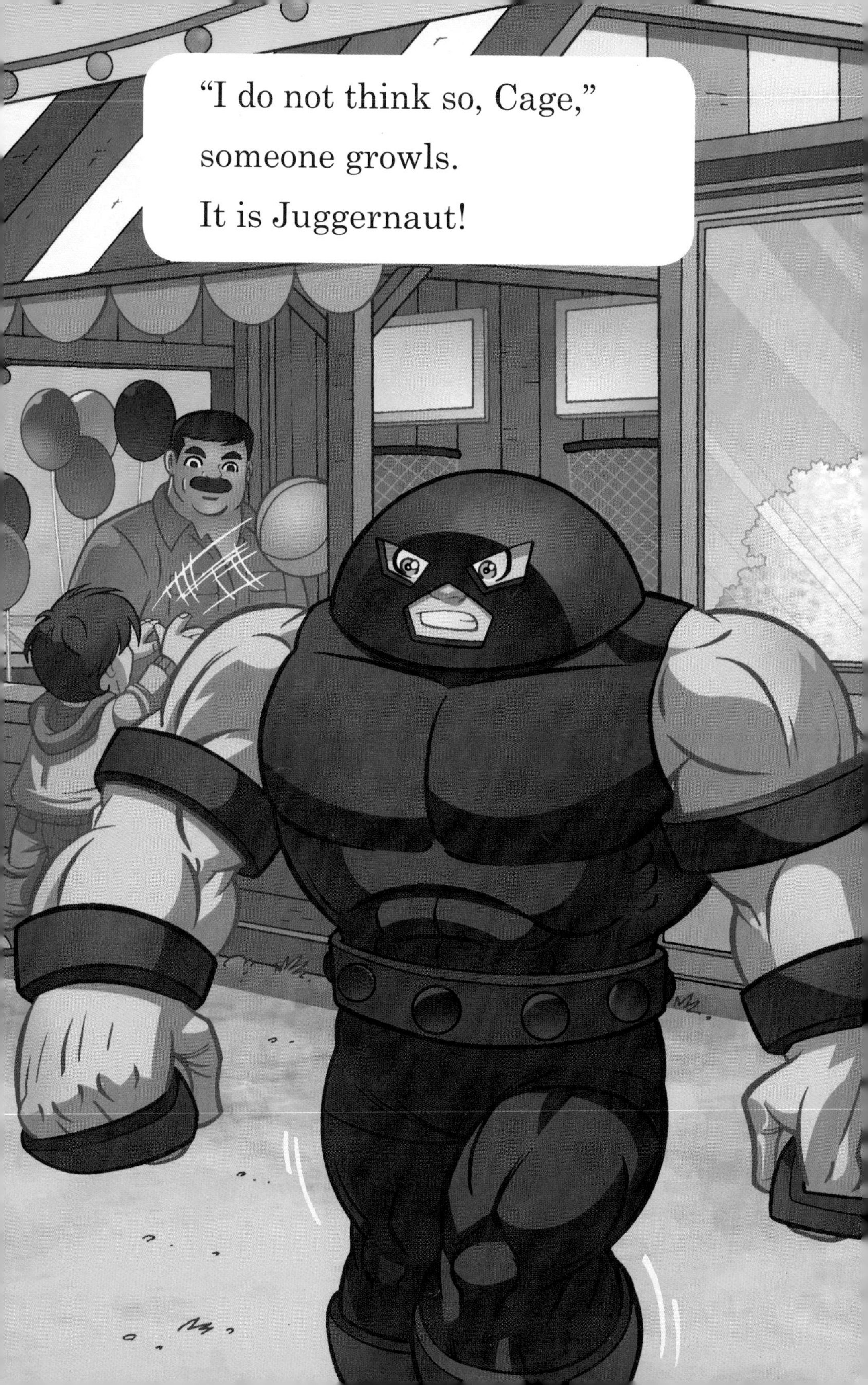

"Let me show you
how it is done,"
says Juggernaut.
He grabs the mallet.
"I was first!" argues Luke.

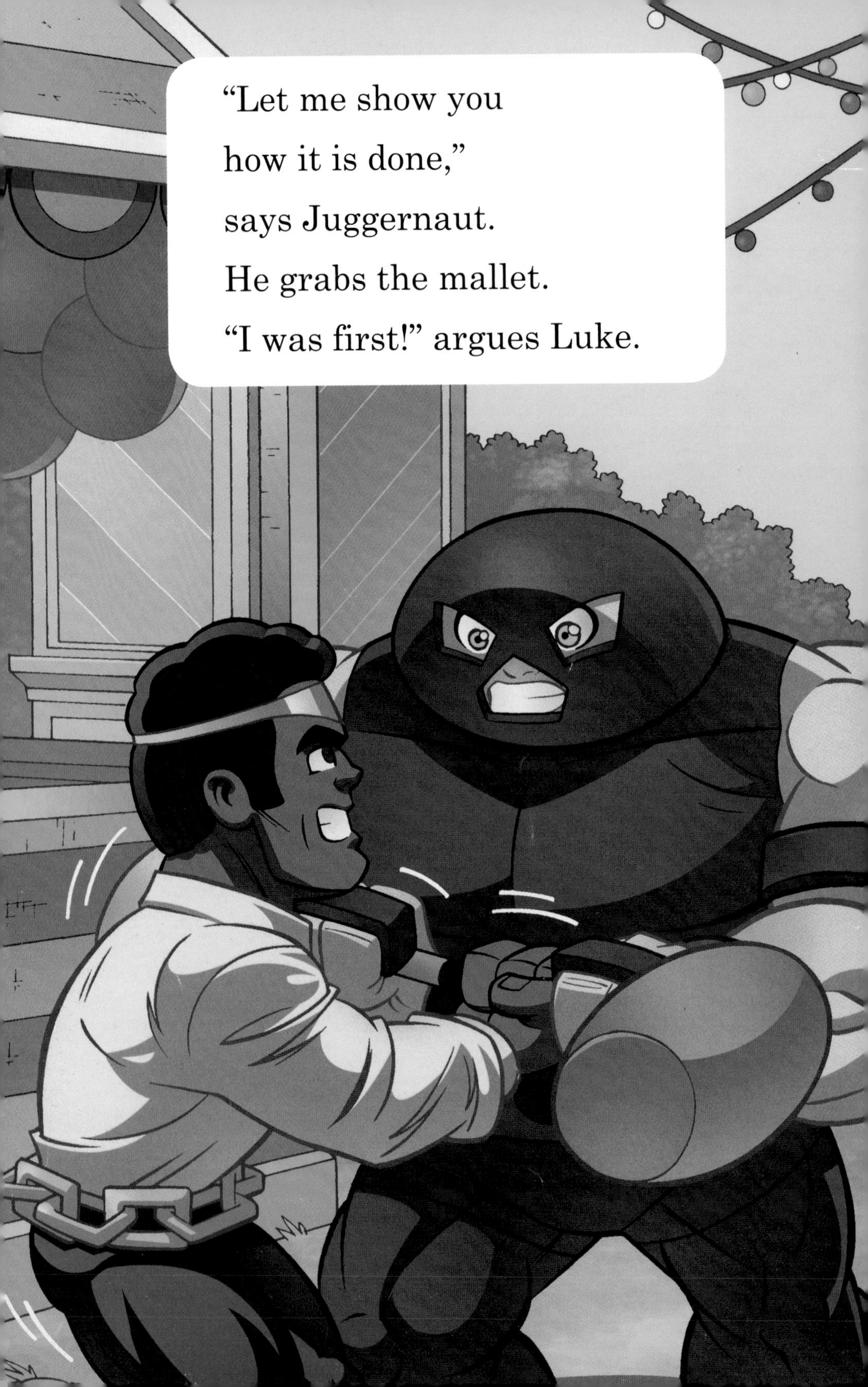

“Be cool,” says Iron Man.
“Today is about having fun.”

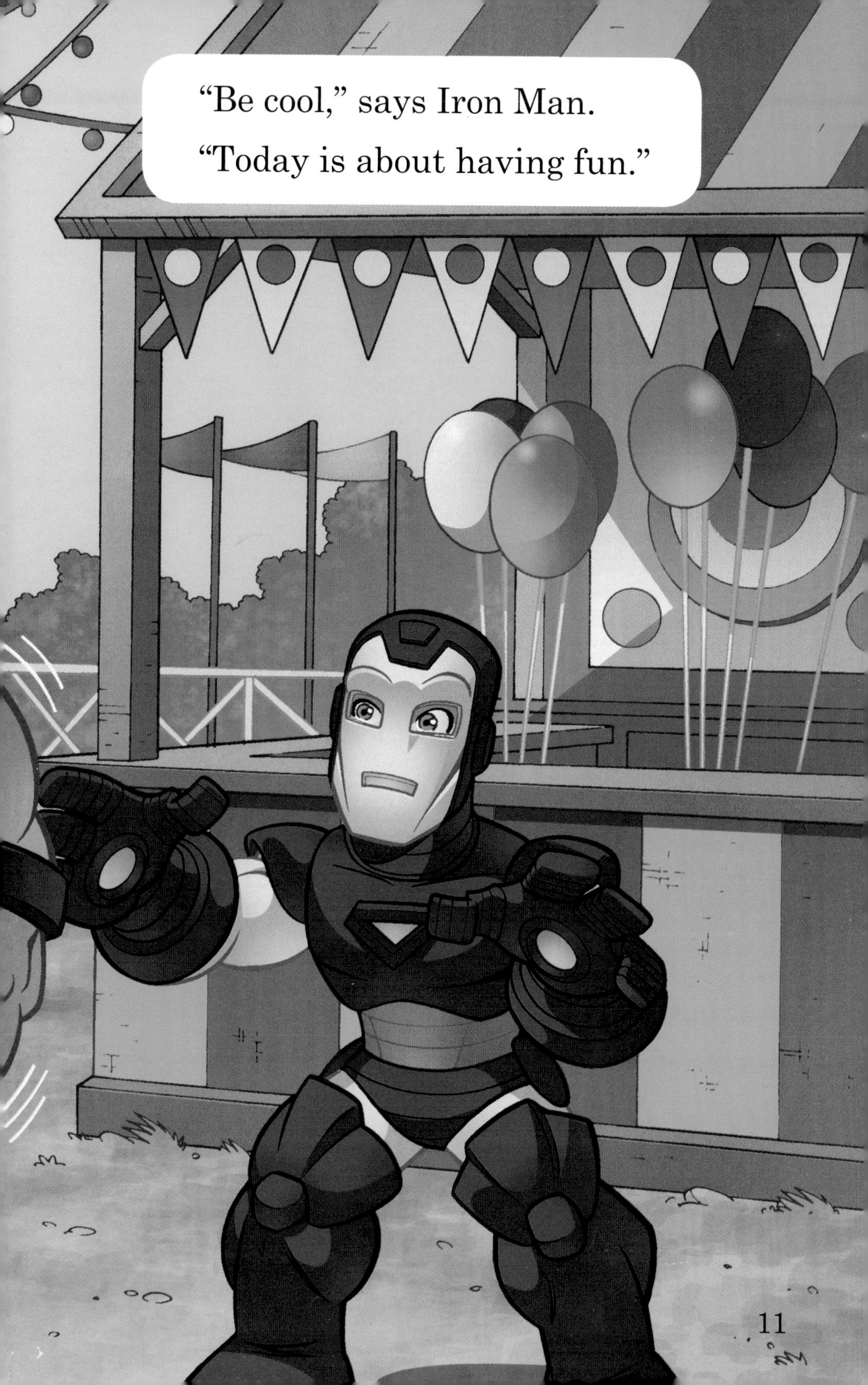

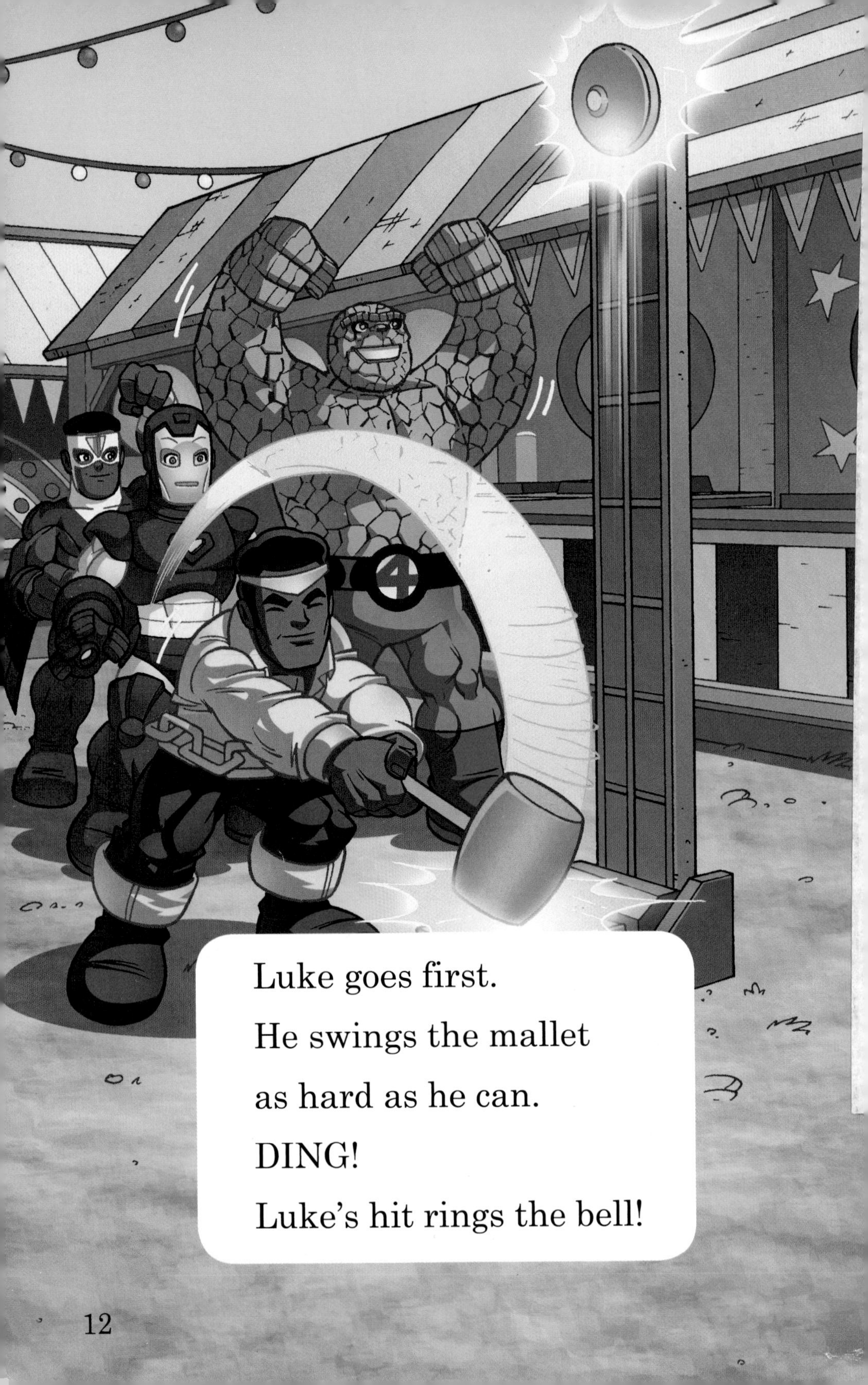

Luke goes first.
He swings the mallet
as hard as he can.
DING!
Luke's hit rings the bell!

“Beat that,” Luke says.
With one swift swing,
Juggernaut hits the bell, too!

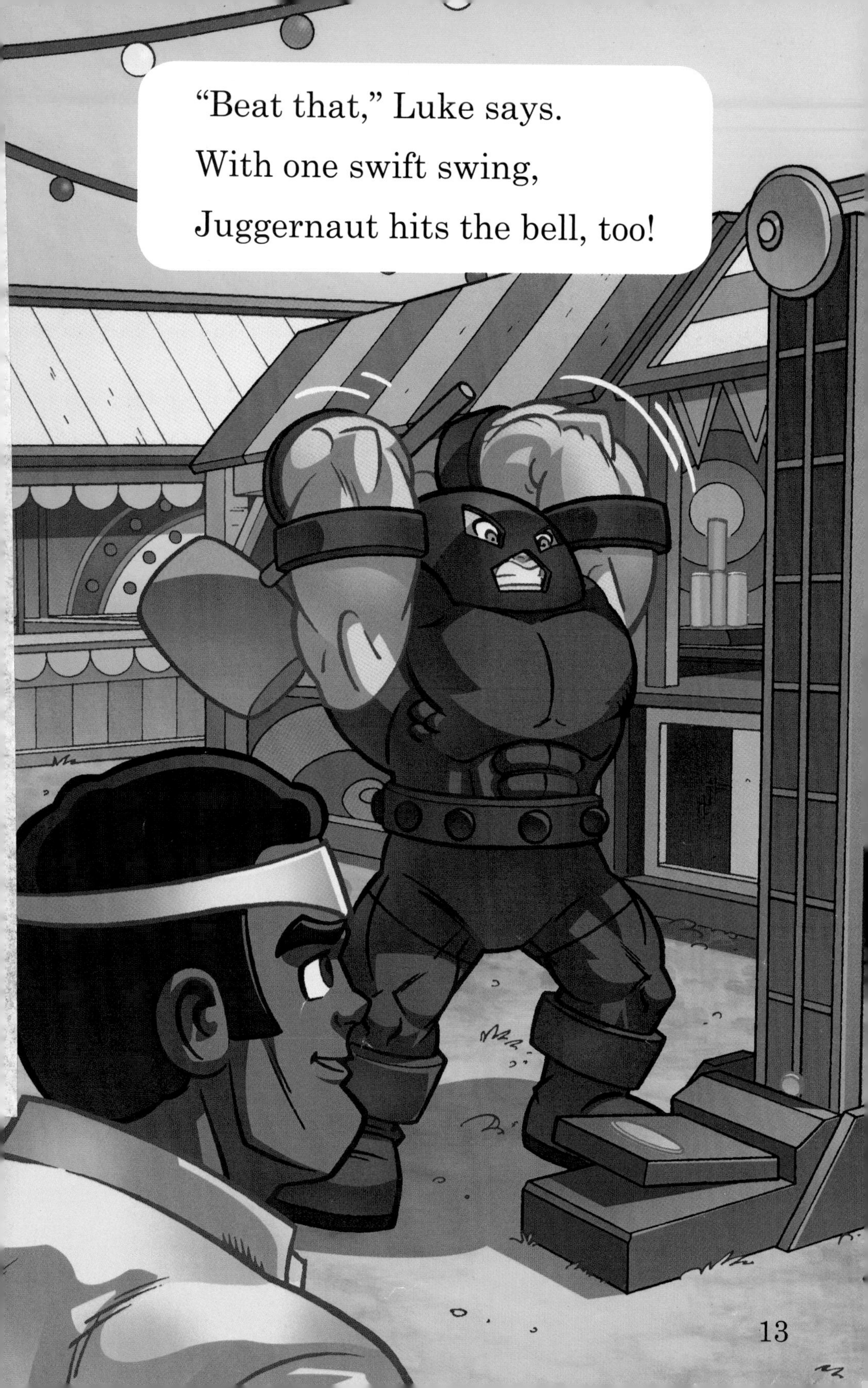

Juggernaut laughs.
"Now who is hot stuff?" he says.

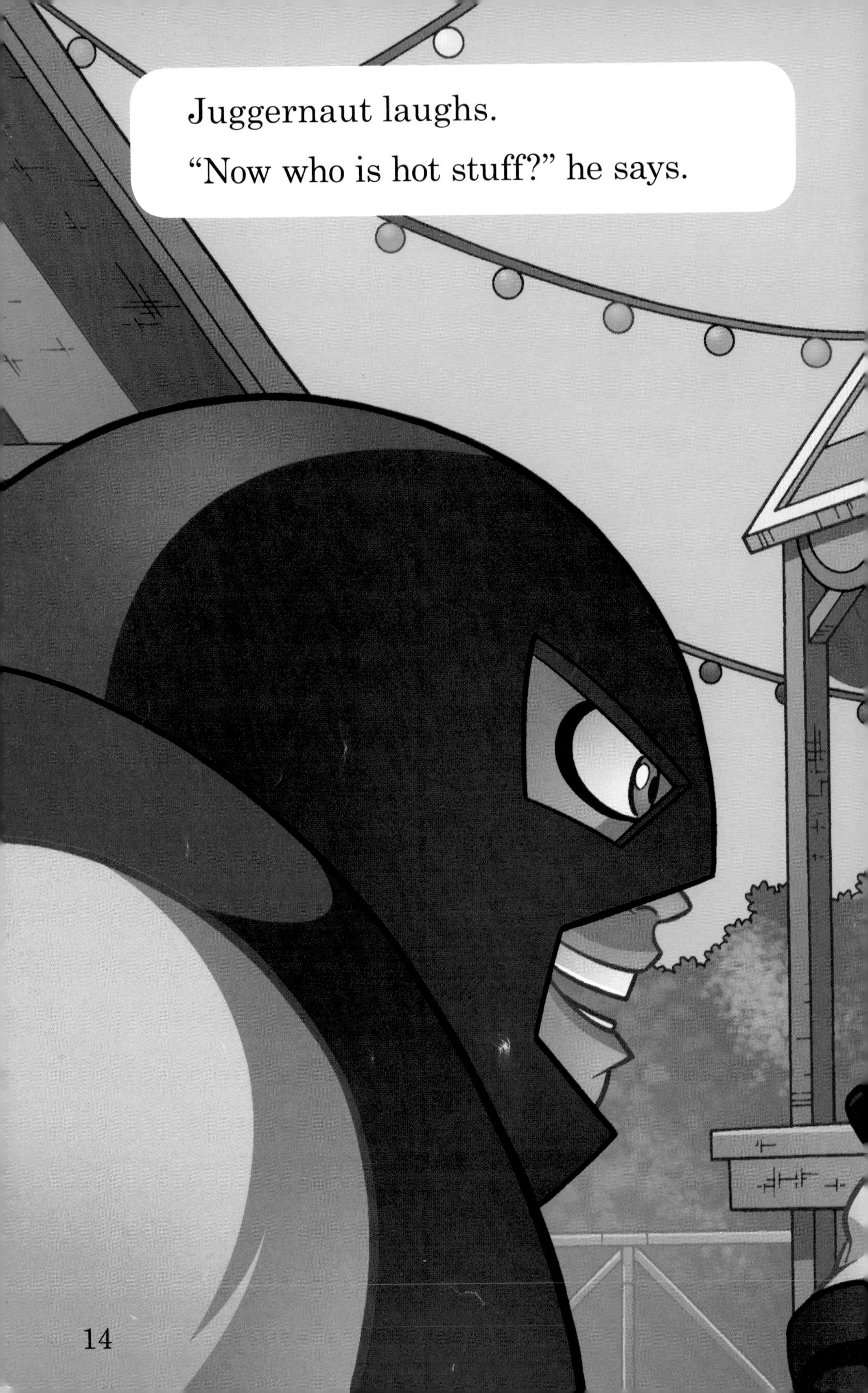

"Anyone can get lucky," says Luke.
"Want to try another contest?
Best two out of three wins!"

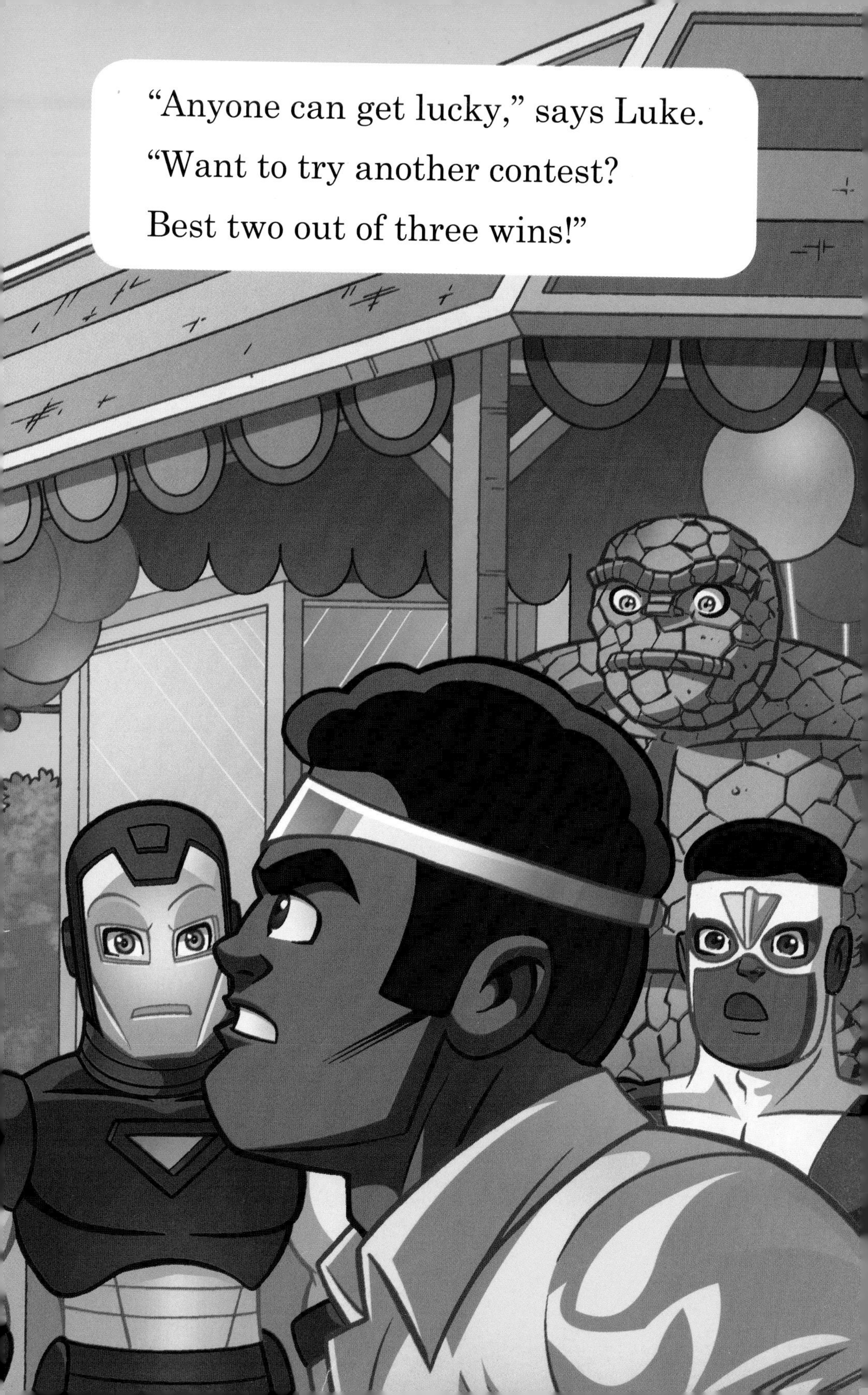

The Squaddies are ready to help.
“Okay, guys,” says Iron Man.
“First up, another strength test.
Who can lift the most?”

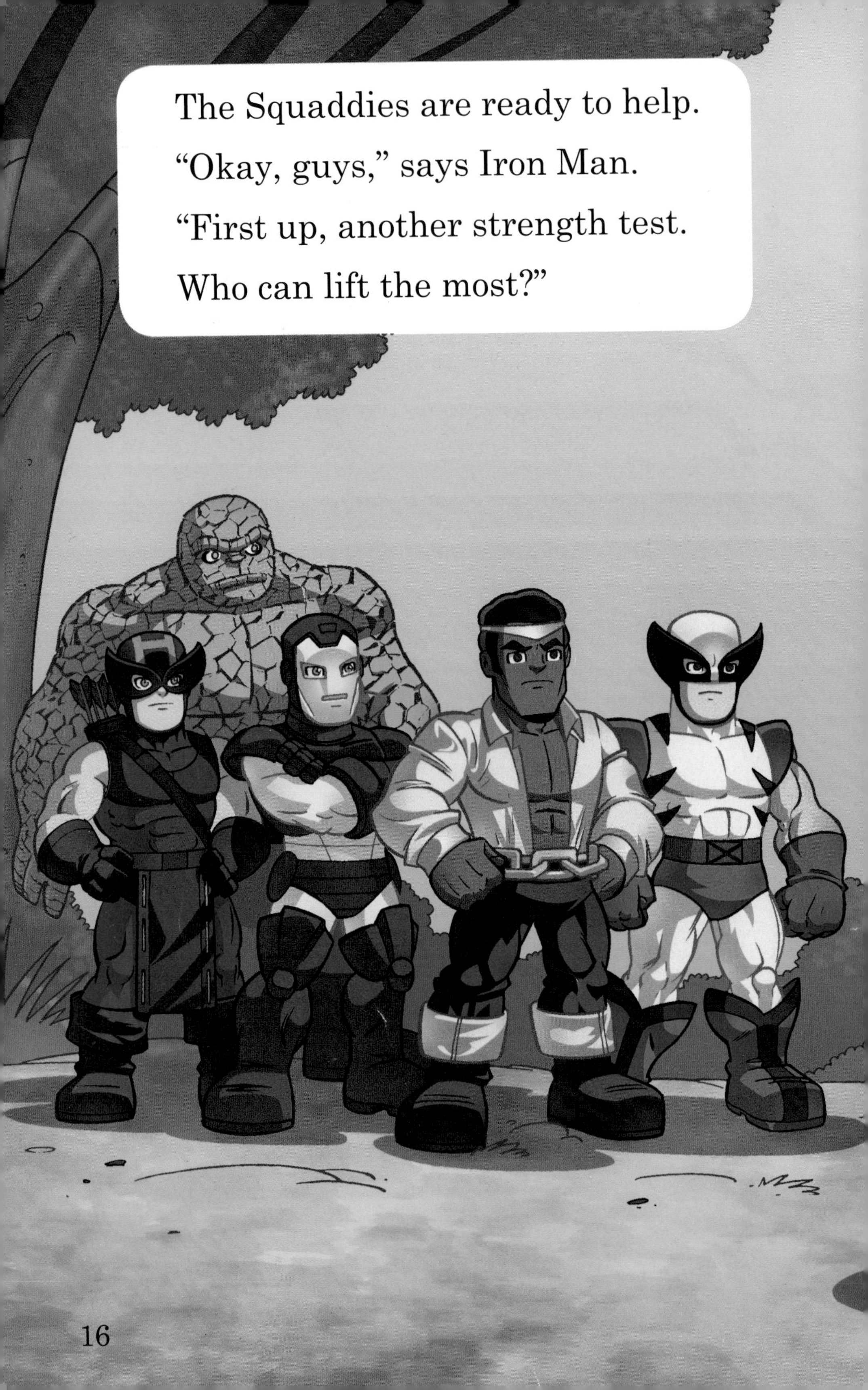

Juggernaut goes first.
He picks up a huge boulder.
“No sweat,” he says.

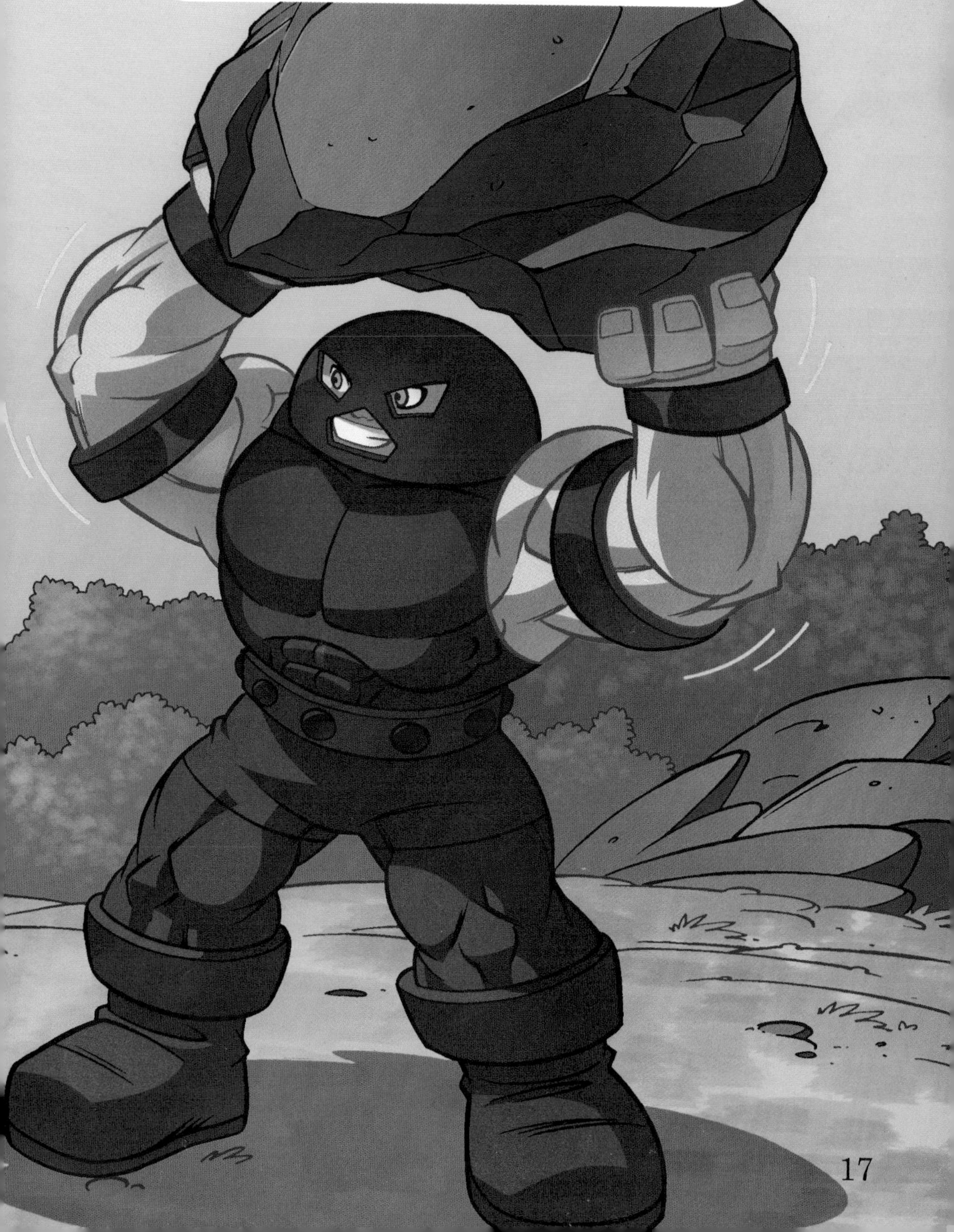

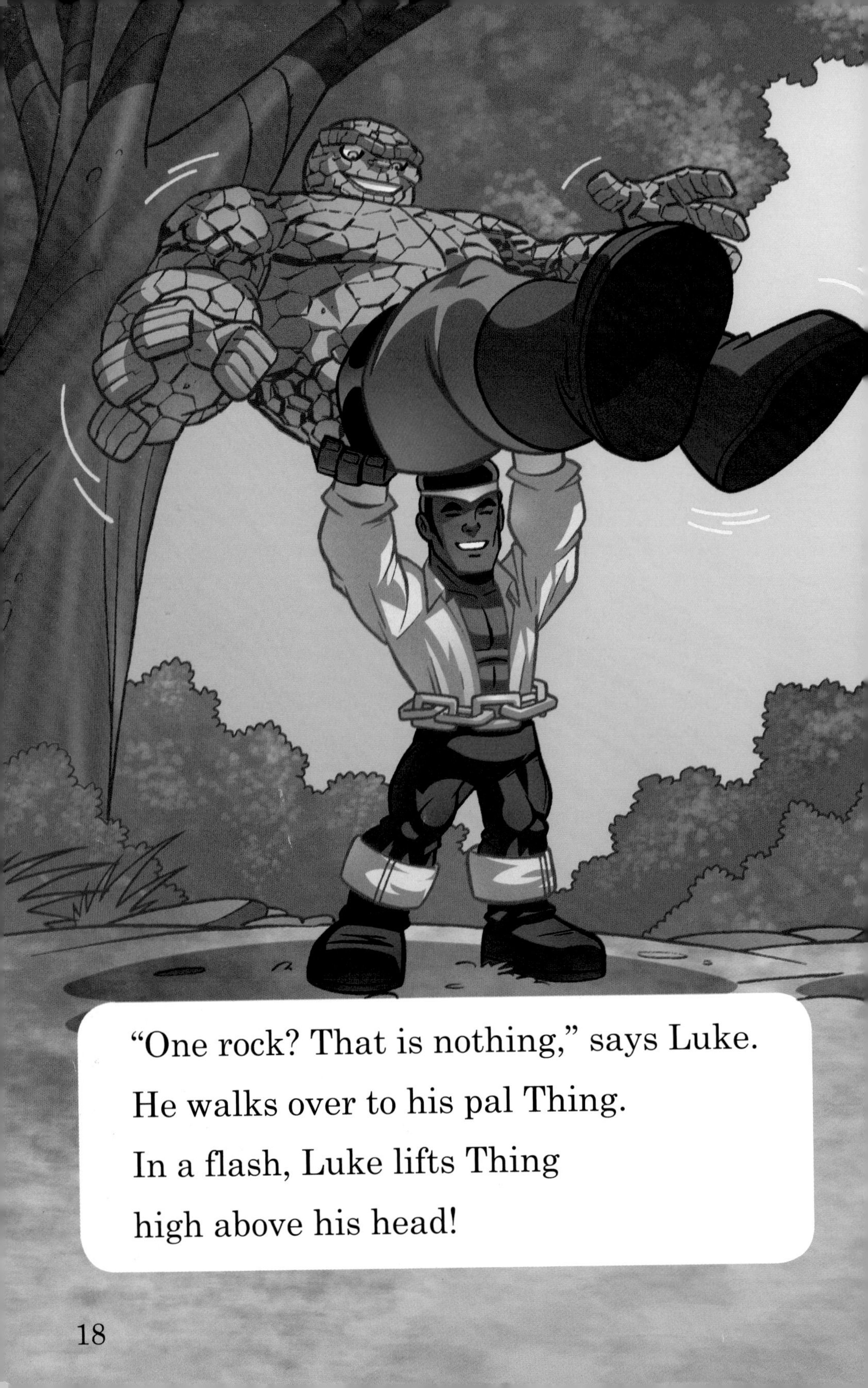

"One rock? That is nothing," says Luke.
He walks over to his pal Thing.
In a flash, Luke lifts Thing
high above his head!

"This guy is like a mountain!" boasts Luke.
"That is true," laughs Iron Man.
"This round goes to Luke Cage!"

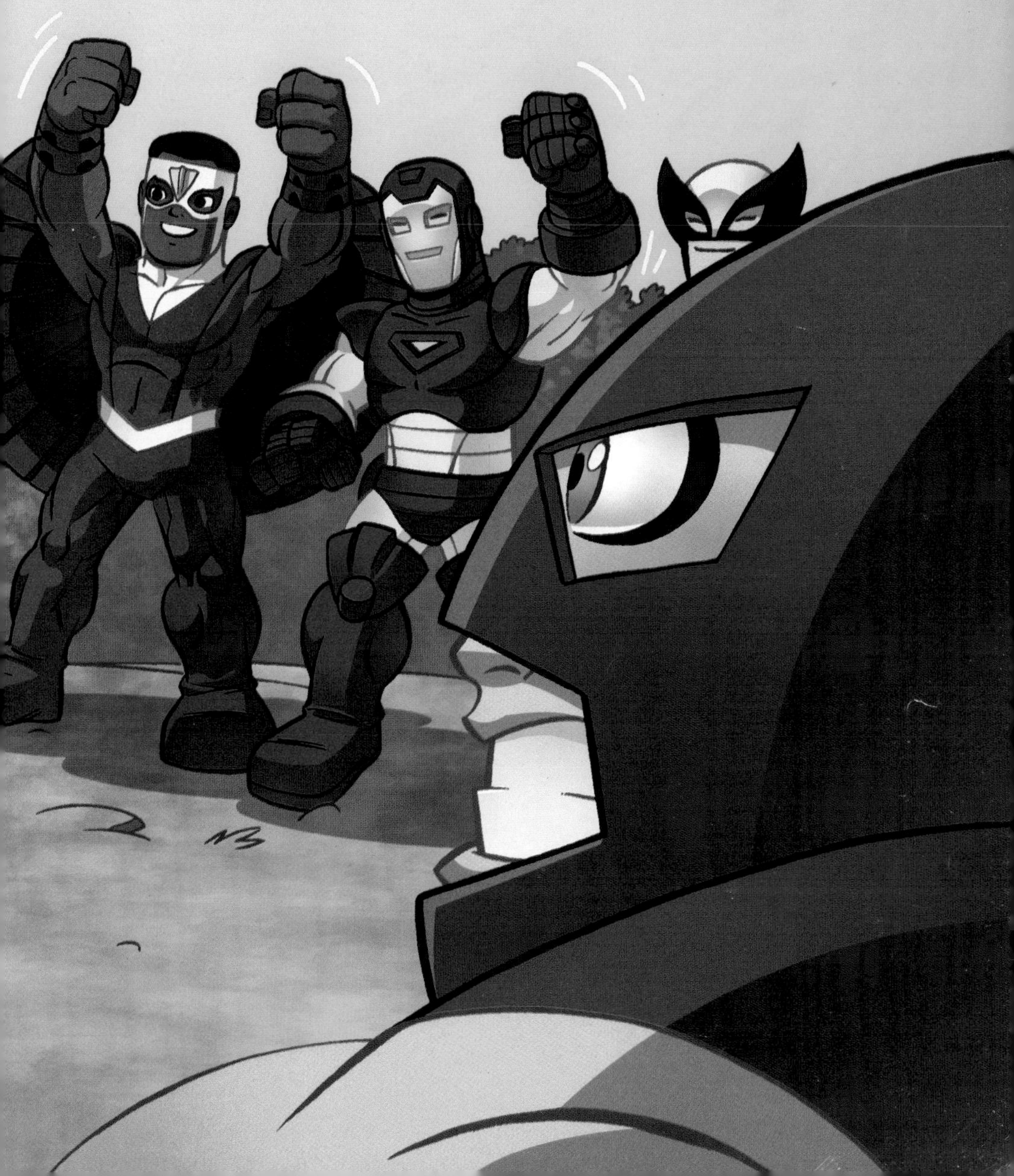

"Next up," says Iron Man,
"a climbing test!
Whoever climbs to the top
of the skyscraper first wins this one."

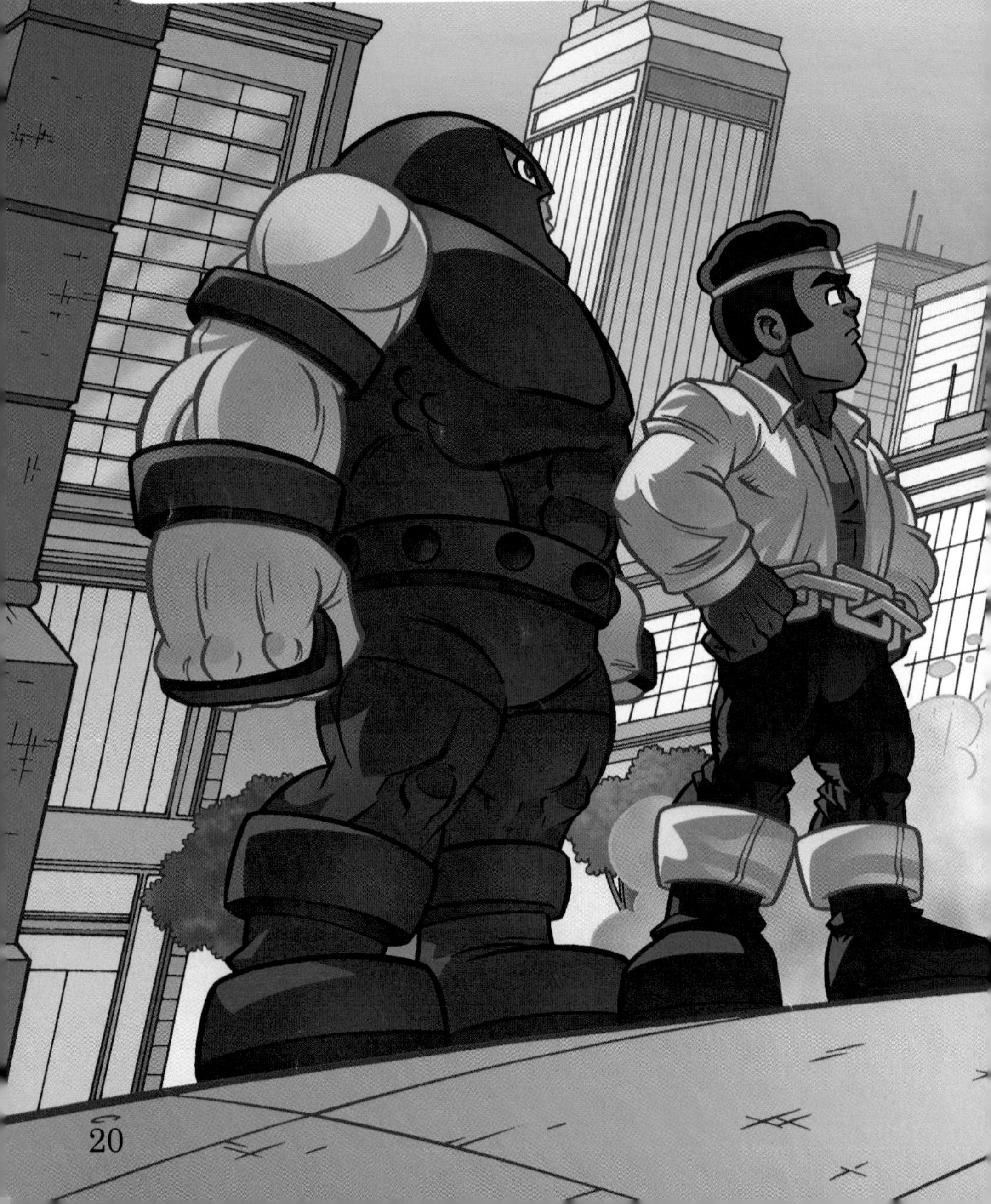

Falcon flies up to the roof.
"On your mark, get set, go!"
he shouts.

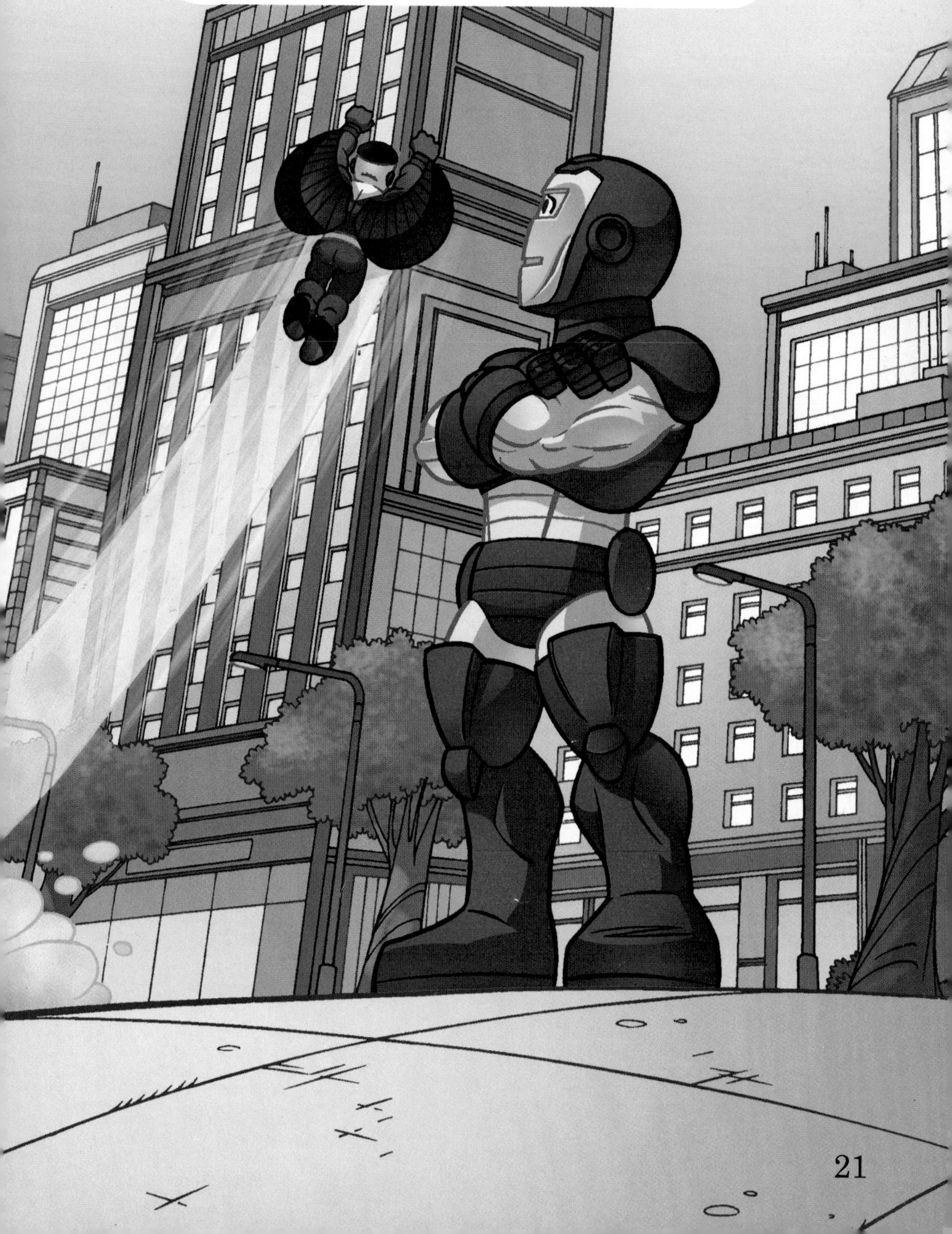

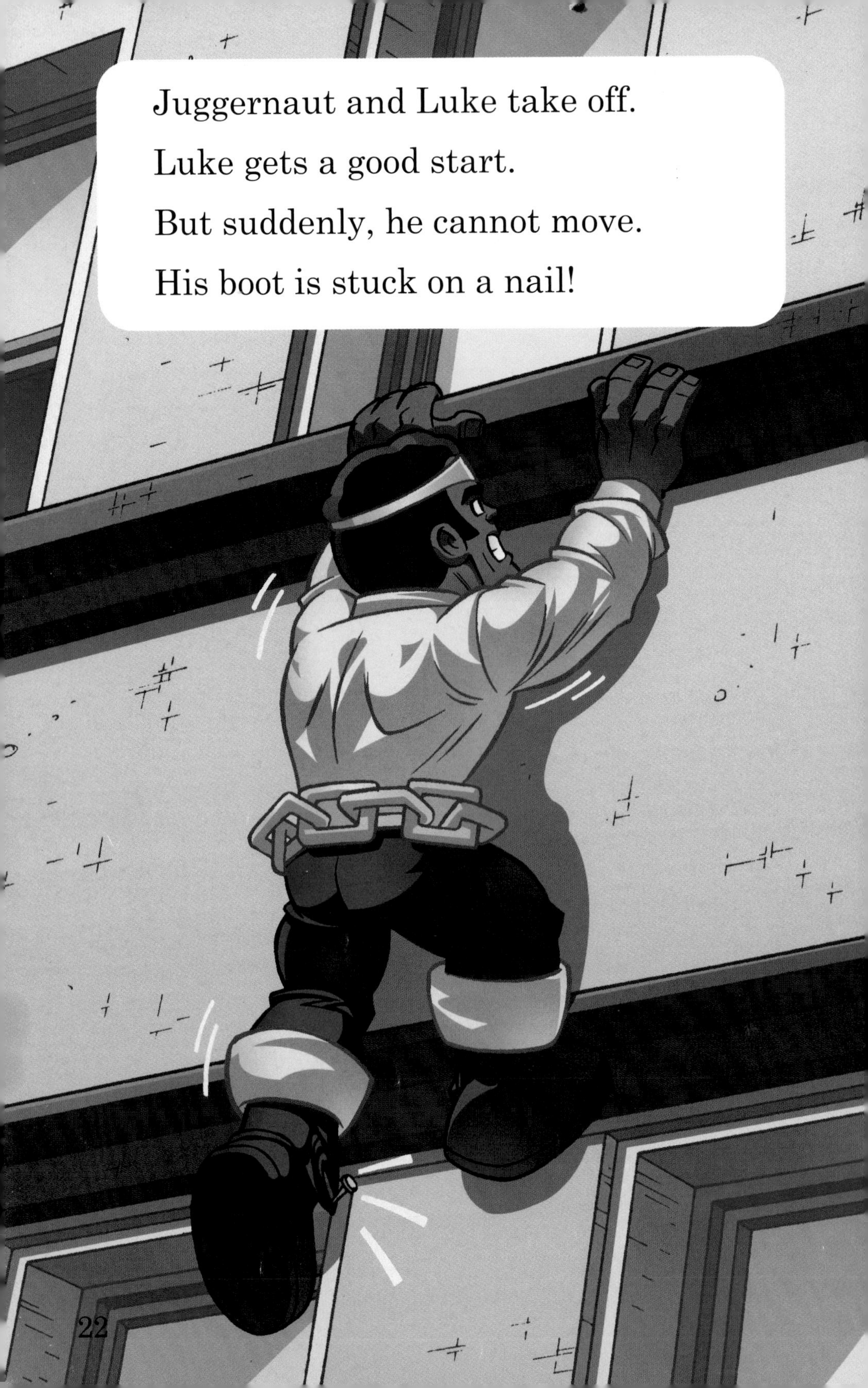
Juggernaut and Luke take off.
Luke gets a good start.
But suddenly, he cannot move.
His boot is stuck on a nail!

Juggernaut takes the lead.
Luke frees himself, but it is too late.
"Juggernaut wins!" cries Falcon.

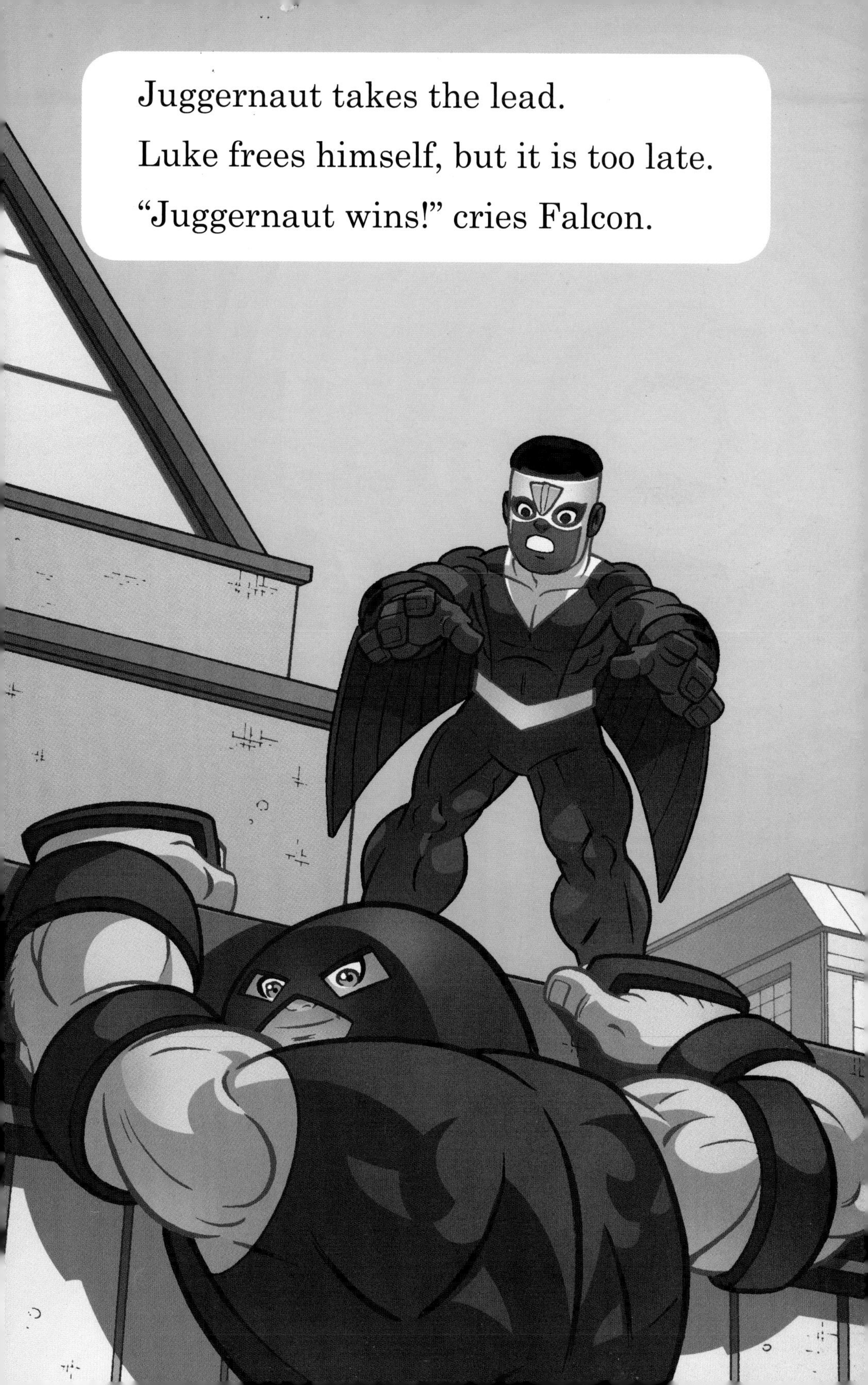

The score is tied.
"Now you have to swim," says Iron Man.
"The first person to swim
across the river wins!"

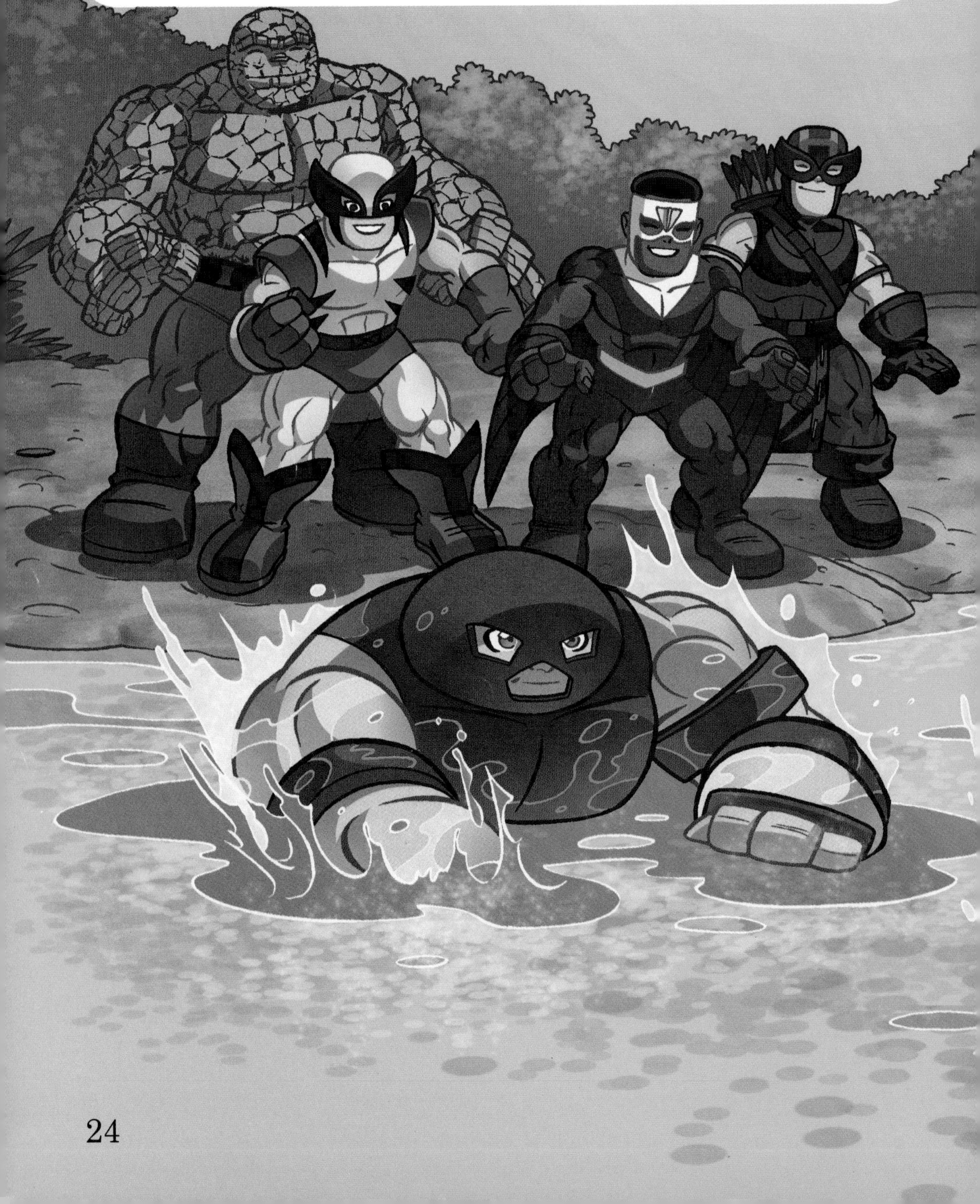

Luke and Juggernaut
dive into the water.
Luke Cage pushes ahead.
He sees the other side
of the river getting closer and closer.

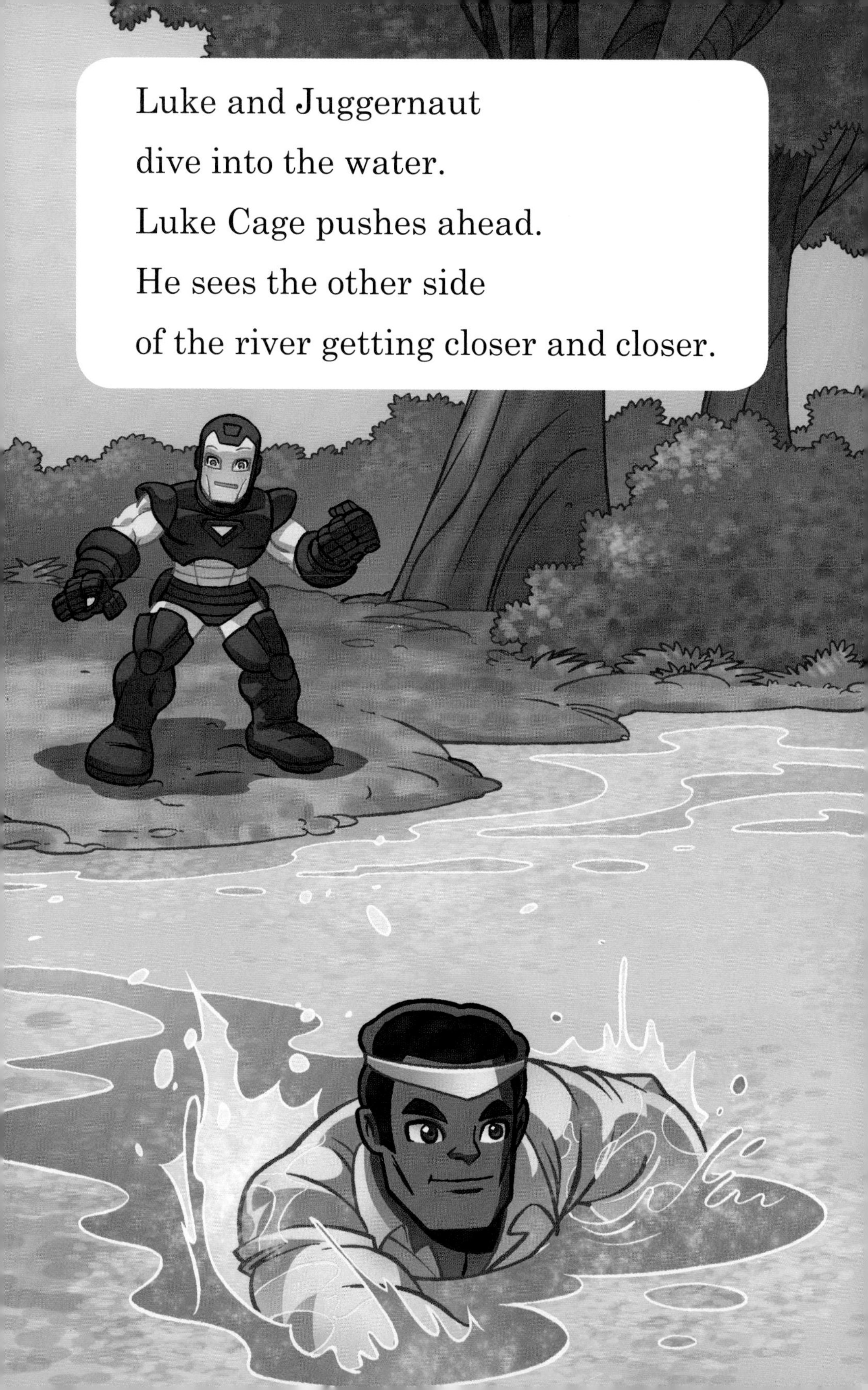

Luke looks back.
Juggernaut is far behind him.
I am going to win! Luke thinks.

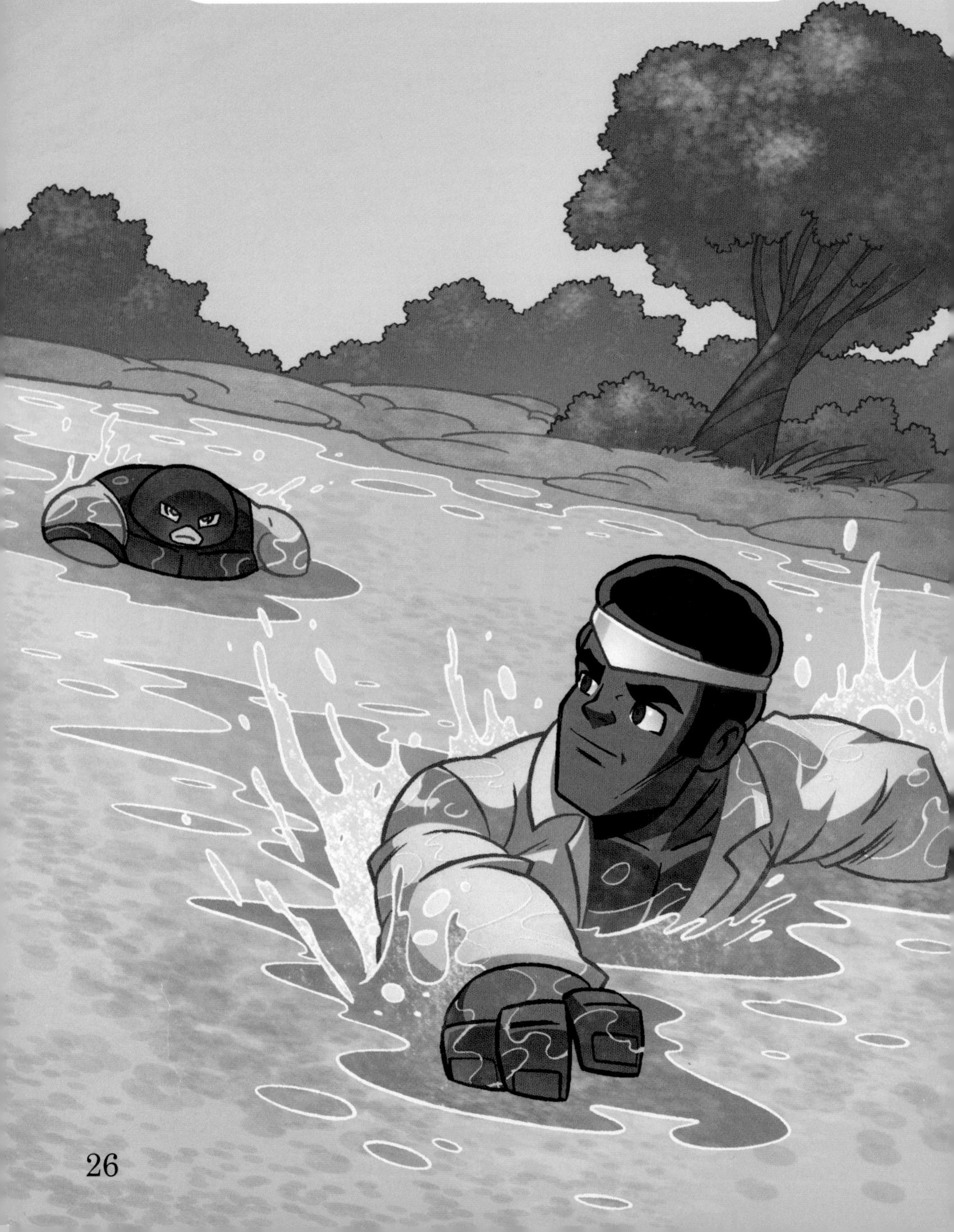

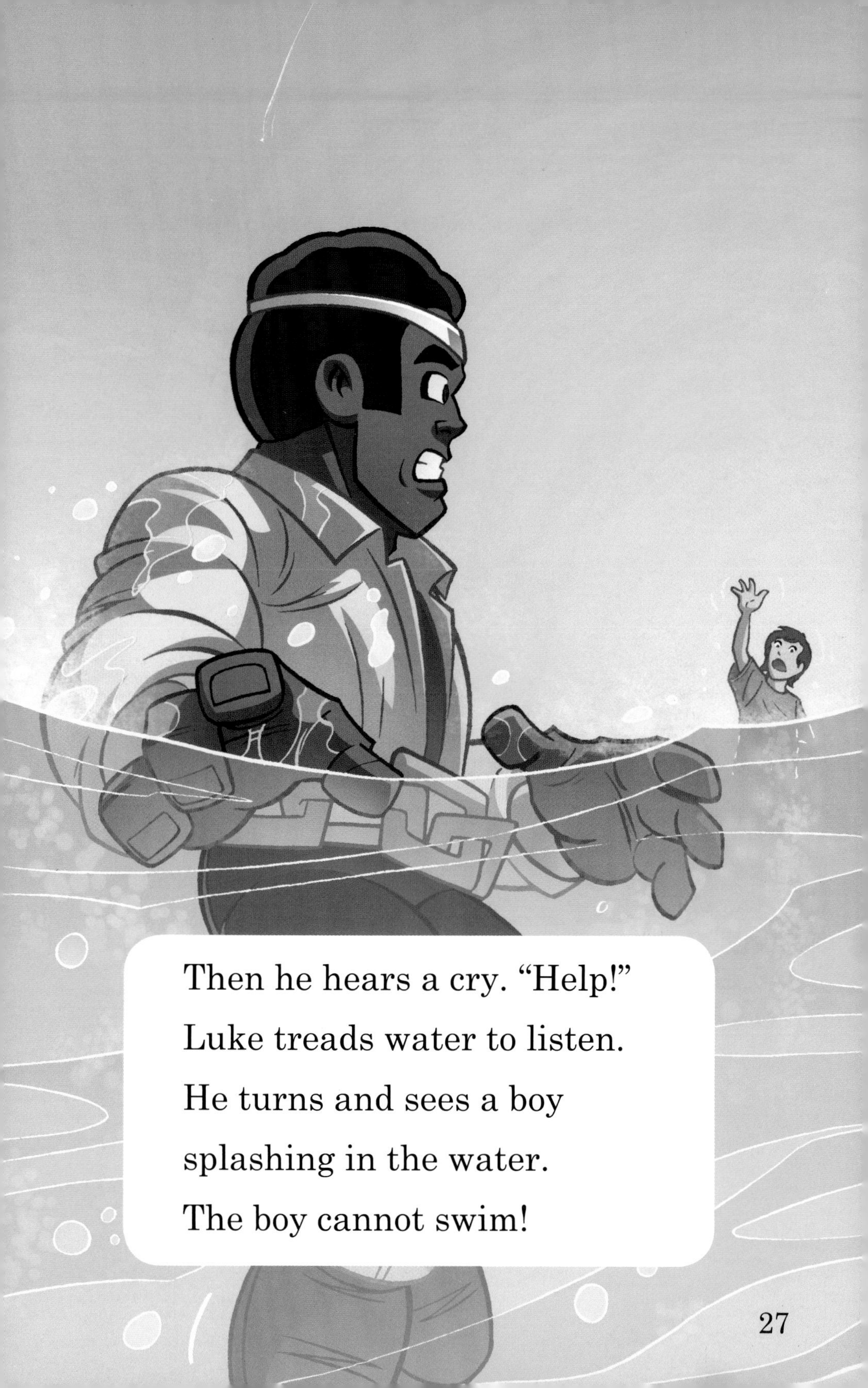

Then he hears a cry. “Help!”
Luke treads water to listen.
He turns and sees a boy
splashing in the water.
The boy cannot swim!

Quickly, Luke swims
to the boy.
He pounds his arms and legs
to swim faster.

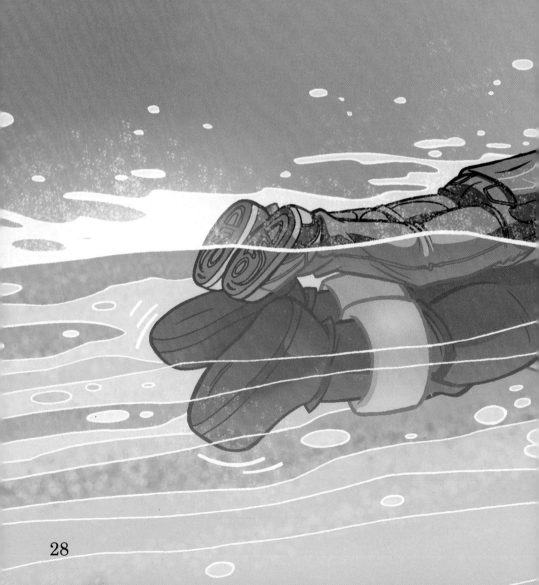

"Got you!" yells Luke
as he pulls the boy
onto his back.
Luke takes him safely
to the shore.

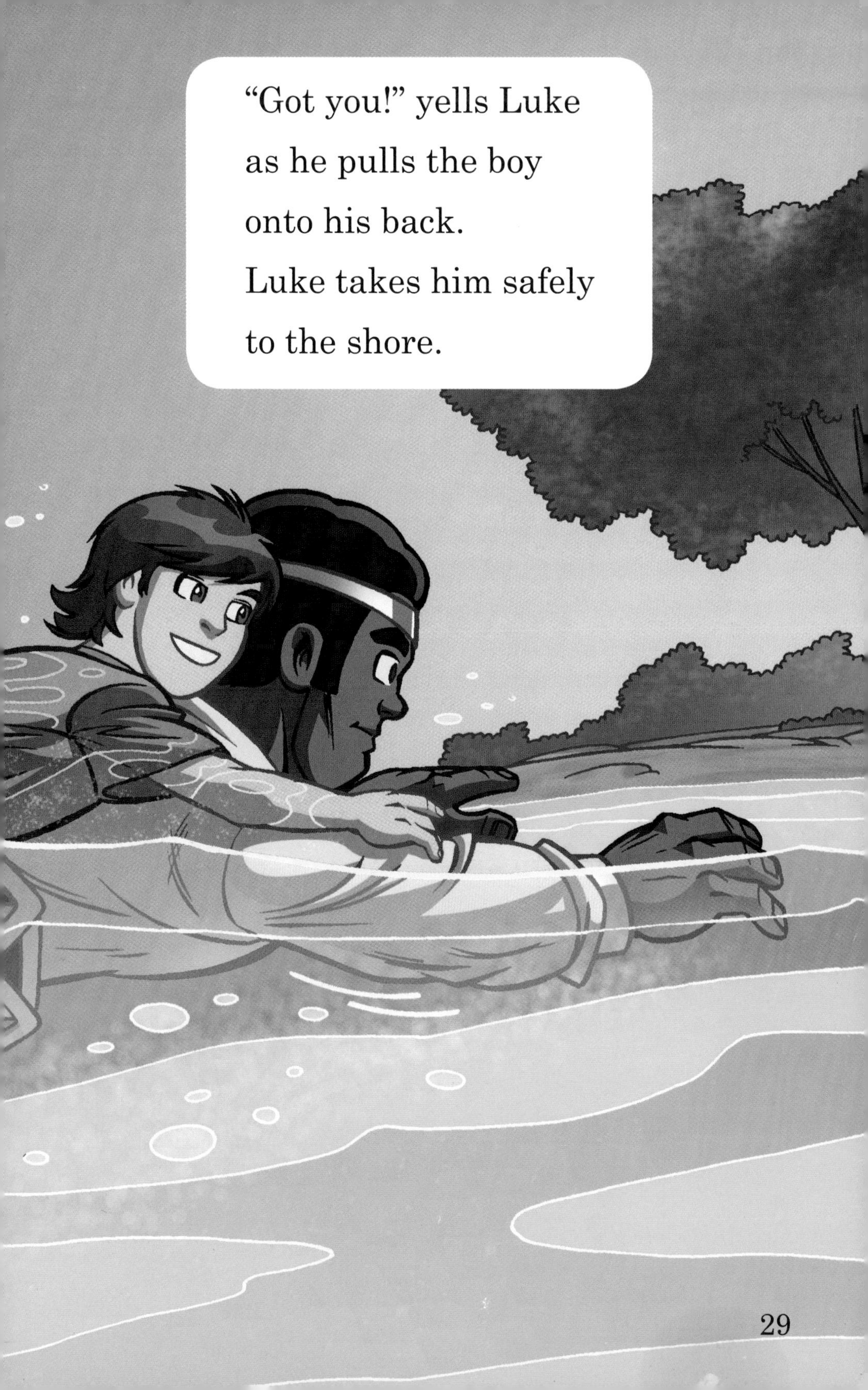

When Luke and the boy
reach the riverbank,
Juggernaut is already there.

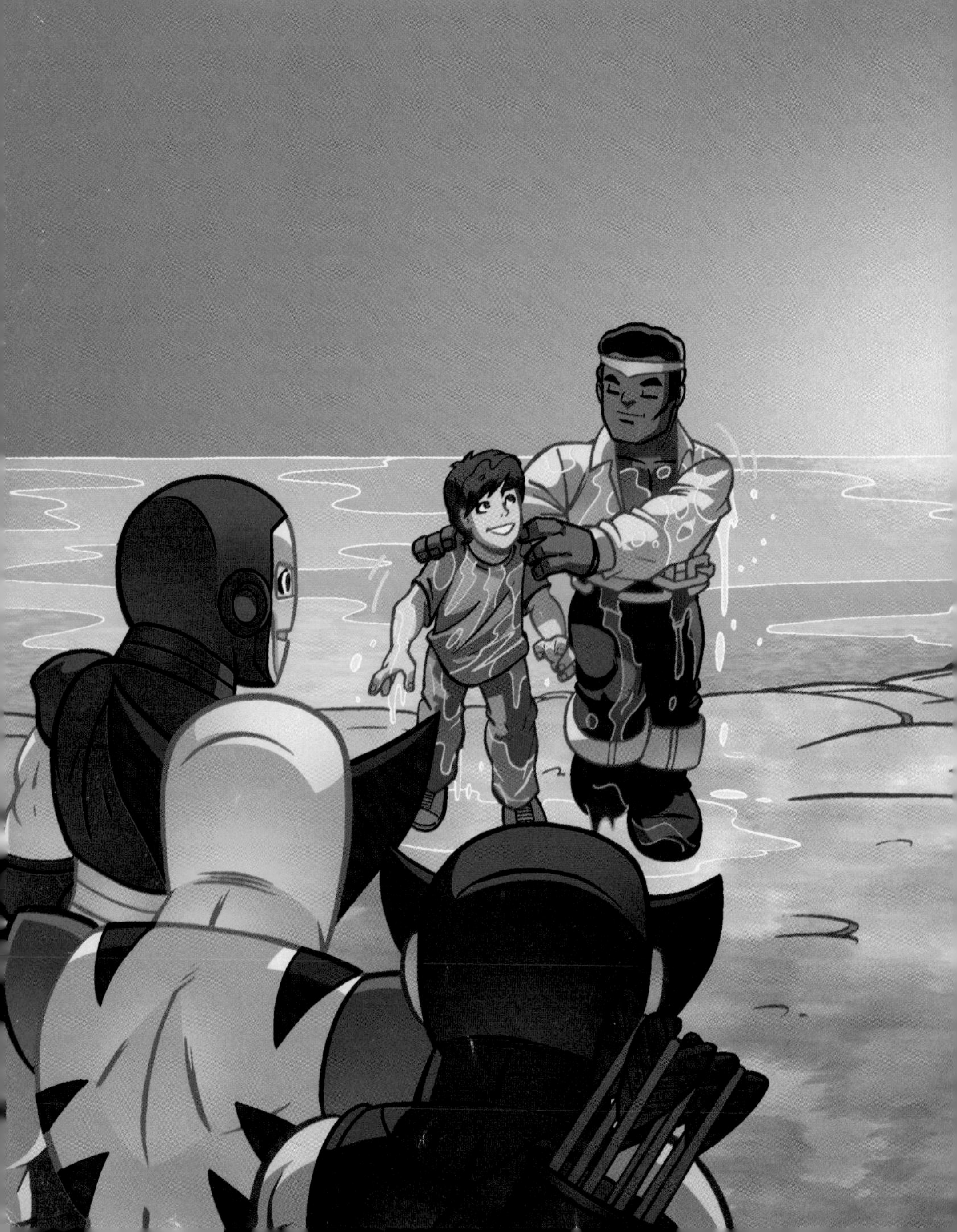

"Looks like you are not the strongest guy around after all," Juggernaut smirks. "I win the contest!"

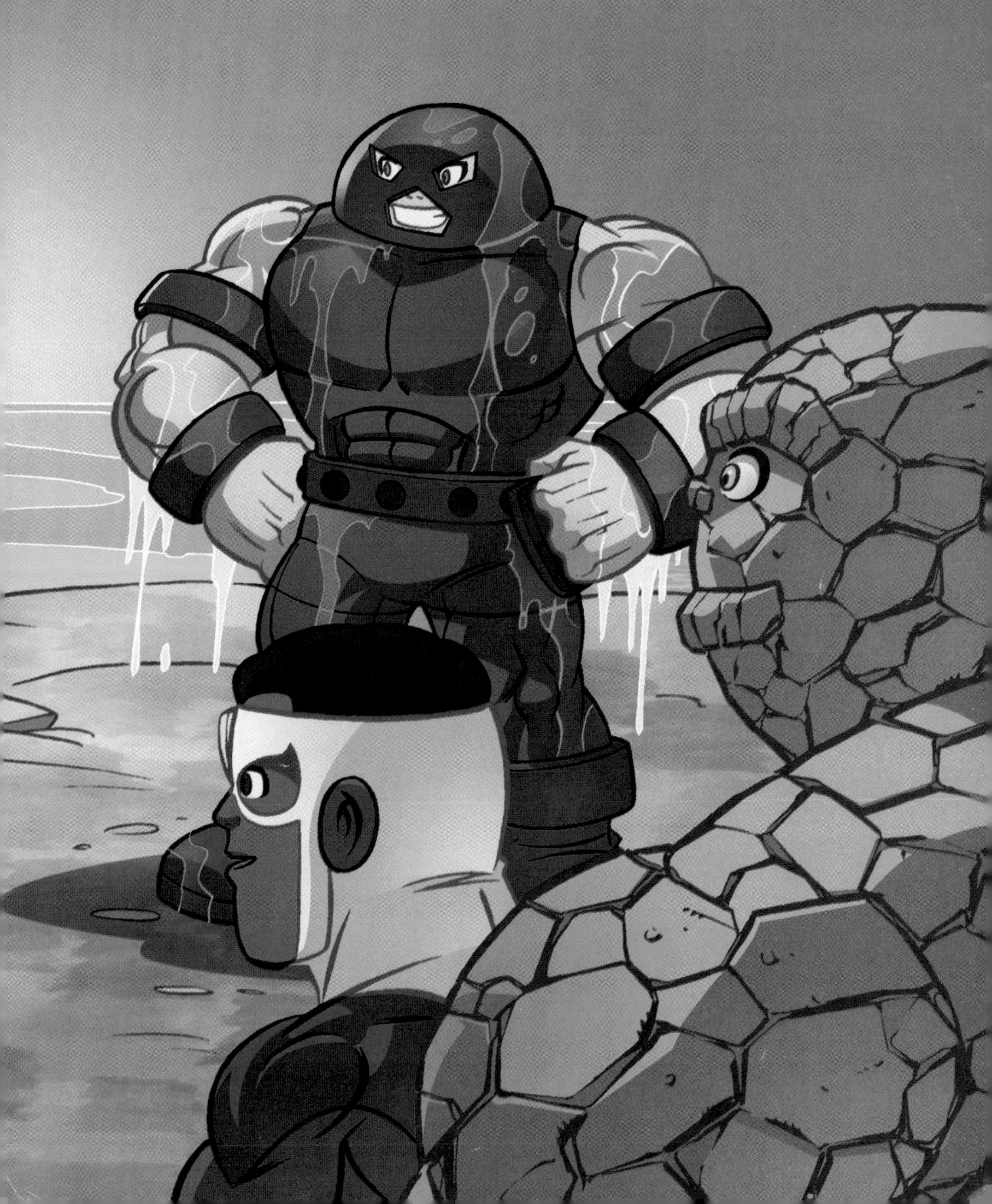

Luke Cage does not mind.
"You might be the winner," he says,
"but I feel like a hero!"

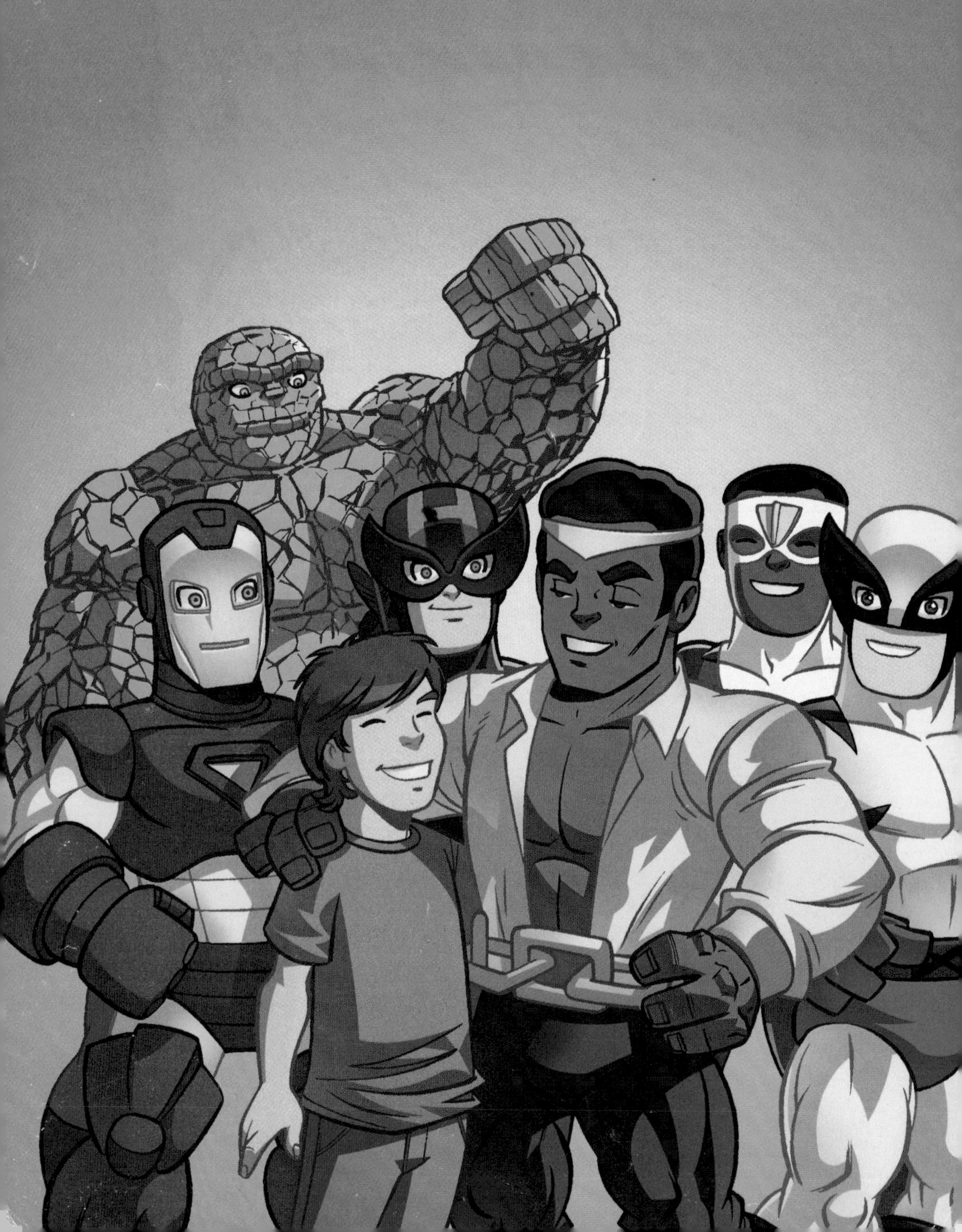